Thanks to Martin, Pam, Paula, Hannah
and Emily and of course Sim and Elsie.

First published 2016 by Macmillan Children's Books
an imprint of Pan Macmillan
20 New Wharf Road, London N1 9RR
Associated companies throughout the world
www.panmacmillan.com
ISBN: 978-1-4472-8769-8 (PB)

Text and illustrations copyright © Julia Woolf 2016

The right of Julia Woolf to be identified as the
author and illustrator of this work has been asserted by her
in accordance with the Copyright, Designs and Patents Act 1988.

5 7 9 8 6 4
A CIP catalogue record for this book is available
from the British Library.

Printed in China

MACMILLAN CHILDREN'S BOOKS

GIRAFFE ON A BICYCLE

Julia Woolf

Monkey found a bicycle.

Luckily, giraffe knew
how to ride it . . .

. . . sort of!

ding!

First they wiggled
one way.

Then they wobbled
the other.

But practice
makes perfect . . .

. . . and off they went!

ding!
ding!

High in the branches,
a stripy tiger was
enjoying a snooze.
But not for long!

"Wakey, wakey,
sleepyhead!"
shouted monkey.
"Join us for some fun!"

So tiger did.

And off they
went, bumpety
bump.

As they pedalled through the trees, three leaping lemurs popped out of the leaves.

"The more, the merrier!" monkey cried.
"Who else will join our jungle ride?"

ding!
ding!

A slithering snake was considering a snack when . . .

"Only us!" monkey chattered.
"Plenty of room for you!"

And before long, a surprised crocodile found he was a passenger too.

"Up you come," giggled monkey. "Make it snappy!"

Down at the lagoon,
a friendly flamingo
wanted to play.

With a flip and a flap, she joined the fun.

As they sped through the vines, three cheeky monkeys dropped from the skies.

Faster! Faster!

ding!
ding!   DING!
DING!

Whooshing through the jungle
was so much fun until . . .

"LOOK OUT!"

shouted monkey.

CRASH!

And up, up, up they went.

"OH NO!"

shouted everybody.

The animals had broken the bicycle!

But luckily
they knew just
how to fix it.

First snake
snatched
the saddle.

Then giraffe
grabbed the
basket.

Everyone knew what to do.

And soon the bike
was as good as new ...

. . . sort of.
And home they went.

ding!